Wild Boys

PRAISE FOR *STORYSHARES*

"One of the brightest innovators and game-changers in the education industry."
– Forbes

"Your success in applying research-validated practices to promote literacy serves as a valuable model for other organizations seeking to create evidence-based literacy programs."

- Library of Congress

"We need powerful social and educational innovation, and Storyshares is breaking new ground. The organization addresses critical problems facing our students and teachers. I am excited about the strategies it brings to the collective work of making sure every student has an equal chance in life."
– Teach For America

"Around the world, this is one of the up-and-coming trailblazers changing the landscape of literacy and education."
- International Literacy Association

"It's the perfect idea. There's really nothing like this. I mean wow, this will be a wonderful experience for young people."   - Andrea Davis Pinkney, Executive Director, Scholastic

"Reading for meaning opens opportunities for a lifetime of learning. Providing emerging readers with engaging texts that are designed to offer both challenges and support for each individual will improve their lives for years to come. Storyshares is a wonderful start."
- David Rose, Co-founder of CAST & UDL

Wild Boys

Kat Jeanette

STORYSHARES

Story Share, Inc.
New York. Boston. Philadelphia

Storyshares
Story Share, Inc.
24 N. Bryn Mawr Avenue #340
Bryn Mawr, PA 19010-3304
www.storyshares.org

Inspiring reading with a new kind of book.

Interest Level: Middle School
Grade Level Equivalent: 3.3

9781642614756

Book design by Storyshares

Printed in the United States of America

Storyshares Presents

1

September 10

I don't belong here. I freaking don't belong here!! This place SUCKS.

#MustGoHomeNOW

#FREEME

2

September 17

The boys here are really bad. A lot of them have rap sheets. One kid even has a baby!!

I don't know why I have to write in a journal. What do I say? Any stupid thing that comes into my brain? What is the point?

Can't believe they stuck me in jail. I need to get out of here. Like, NOW.

We have to get up way too early: 6 AM! The food in the chow hall is actually pretty okay. But every day is the same snack at 10:30. A person can only eat so many apples and granola bars. AND we only get to eat at meal times. Some boys said they know how to sneak into the refrigerators, but they won't tell how. I can't figure that out because the Direct Care staff guards us 24/7.

I wonder why Ezra didn't come when they dumped me here...

3

September 24

I don't know why Mom and Dad are making me be here. We were having a nice vacation. I should have known something was up that last day, when Ezra refused to come with us to check out a college for Casey. Dad bribed me to go by saying we could eat at a fancy steakhouse.

Which we did. But after all that driving, when we finally pulled up to the buildings — it didn't look like any college to me. I would've run away if I knew.

It still creeps me out, thinking about it. Mom was ugly crying after all those guys in army outfits surrounded the car. I didn't even want to look at her. Dad was kind of stiff, or something. And Casey turned so all I saw was her hair. I tried to get out of the car but this huge guy — Mr. Todd, I know now, because he's one of the Direct Cares — made everyone get out of the car except me.

He talked to Dad and Mom for a long time and then told me to get out and stand spread eagle. I did, but he said, "Turn around, you're not getting arrested. You're in a program for 18 months and you have to say 'yes, ma'am' and 'yes, sir.' You got that?"

And I said, "Yeah" and he said, "Yes, sir."

"Yessssss, sirrrrrr."

Then he patted me down. They stood all around me in a circle and made me walk into the building in my socks. I remember thinking, *How can the sunset be so nice when this is so horrible?*

I haven't seen Mom or Dad or Casey since then. I am real sad because I miss them so much, but at the same time I hate their guts.

Plus there are no girls here — that's whacked!

CADET,

We've been doing this for a long time. We know what works and what doesn't. You'll understand in time.

–Pastor Fred

4

October 1

Dad's birthday was yesterday. I wish I was there. I'd like to get him a new grill. Ours is all rusted and a wheel is missing. I wonder if they had a cookout without me.

I am starving for good food. I dream of BBQ potato chips! And beef jerky!

Three boys left the program. I can't use names, so here are the reasons why:

#1 - turned 18 and signed himself out.

#2 – his grandparents who raised him want him closer to home because the grandpop is very ill.

#3 – disappeared one day. That's just how it goes sometimes. Poof. Gone.

5

October 8

I am so tired. They work us all day long.

In drills, we have to stand perfectly still for hours until every last kid shuts up. There's always some lamebrain who won't. We march everywhere. We have to go to chapel every morning, but I can hardly keep awake.

I have no idea where we are. Santi, Texas, but where on a map? I heard someone say that it's God's country, so I guess God likes it hot and dusty. If there is a God.

I have blisters on my feet because these boots are like wearing bricks.

I really miss my friends. They're probably wondering what happened to me. I want to tell Mom to text some of them and tell them I'm away but will be back soon. She doesn't like too many of them because she thinks they're bad and that they like me for the wrong reasons. CLUELESS, Mom.

CADET

Your parents have been advised not to contact your friends.

– Pastor Fred

6

October 15

I'm allowed to get a phone call with Dad and Mom next week. I've been thinking for a long time about what to say. There is so much. I'm not sure if I will cry, or maybe I will get angry and not speak to them. I don't know what they're thinking. Maybe they will cry or yell at me. I wish I could talk to Ezra, but they said that won't happen for a long time.

They also said no personal items allowed. But I would really like to have my slippers. When I get home, they might not fit anymore.

Vasquez has the bunk under mine. He's pretty quiet. I like that. He's from Texas, somewhere. He said his mom hardly speaks any English, so she just nods when staff talk to her. He has to translate sometimes. I knew Spanish, once. But I forgot all of it.

There's this other kid — Balacone — I hate him and he's such an idiot. He sticks his bad breath in my face and dares me to do stupid stuff and then laughs. One of these days, I'm gonna shove his teeth back in his head so hard.

I'm not gonna make it here.

CADET,

Threats are strictly prohibited and subject to write-up. Consider this your final warning. Reference to another cadet by name is not allowed in this journal, either.

– Pastor Fred

7

October 22

Had my first phone call with Mom and Dad. It's been six weeks! It went okay. I didn't really know what to say. (I only thought about it for six weeks!) I really wanted to know how come Ezra didn't say goodbye or come on the drive here. They said he was so upset that he couldn't face coming.

They didn't say YES when I asked if I could come home. But when they visit in December, I can probably change their minds.

A tropical storm came through this week. Some boys from another program came and stayed in sleeping bags in the chapel. And then some men from an addiction center were shipped in and stayed in the gym. We are the only place around that has really strong concrete walls, so people who live in flimsy places can come here.

I was surprised that the Direct Cares stayed with us. I thought they'd go home to their families. I would! Maybe they got paid a lot of money to stay.

It was a little bit exciting. It's just that nothing big ever happens here. Every day is kind of the same. Except on Sunday we can watch movies if we didn't get in too much trouble that week. The movies are kind of lame, though, being G-rated.

8

October 29

This kid came in last week, he said he's from Montana and that his dad is a millionaire. I can't even remember his last name, it's so long. He's got a big scar across his eyebrow and he's huge, like 6'4". But he's soft. I could probably take him.

Every day at lunch and dinner he says stuff to me like, "Look out Mama, it's The Bean Bandit." He does it real sneaky, so the Direct Cares don't hear him.

One time in chapel, he was rapping at me under his breath. Over and over. One word. I don't know why he's gotta do that. I'm not even sure what the word means, but I can tell it's bad.

I told Mr. Janson, the DC on duty. The kid said he didn't do it. So it was me against him. Mr. Janson made us go in a room and talk it out and shake hands. But I know he's gonna do it again.

They told us that 74 boys are in the program right now. That's a lot, but I've been here almost 2 months and don't know anybody's first name. I can barely remember my own. Oh, right — Max.

I ain't gonna make it here.

9

November 5

Man! I missed tricker treating! Getting all that C-A-N-D-Y! Mrs. T-Bone — she's in charge of the kitchen — put some candy on each of our dinner trays. But I missed getting a whole bucket full of giant chocolate bars and stuff.

I've been thinking a lot about what I put Dad and Mom and Ezra and Casey though. I did some bad things and put a lot of holes in walls. I hope they can forgive me.

Dad is old and he should retire and have some fun. Get a sailboat. He used to talk about buying all of us matching boat captain hats and sailing around the Finger Lakes. That hat idea was so dumb. He'd been saying he'd retire when his birthday rolled around.

But since his birthday was three weeks after I got hijacked here, I don't know what exactly happened.

CADET,

"Tricker treating" is spelled wrong, but we're not big on that sport anyway. If you get a good evaluation this week, I will bring you a Texas-sized candy bar at next session.

– Pastor Fred

10

November 12

Going crazy with no electronics. Not even a TV, which I hardly ever watched at home anyway. No cell, no computer, no nothing.

My birthday is in two months. I hope they let me out by then. You don't get any presents here and no one can visit you. I hate it here. I'm DONE.

CADET,

You're supposed to be writing a whole page. Please try to focus on some positive or reflective aspects of your daily living.

– Pastor Fred

11

November 19

Reflect... reflect... oh well.

Speaking of reflections (haha) we're not allowed to look in a mirror until we get promoted. Come on!

The guys who have been here a while said there's a pizza shop not far from here, and on Parent Weekend your parent can buy lunch there. If they have cheesesteaks, here is what I want on mine:

- American cheese
- fried onions

- ketchup
- tiny bit of mustard

There was an outdoor baptism this morning. It is funny to me because the baptized kid used to get in a lot of fights, but then he started being pretty good and reading his Bible. He goes around saying "You sinned! You're a sinner!" when kids are bad, so he is not very popular.

I wish I could text my friends. It's like the dark ages here.

#FREEMAX

12

November 26

I have been very sad. On Thanksgiving it is not good to be away from your family. I got a seven-minute call, but that's it.

I miss the fam and all my friends. I hope they all enjoyed a good turkey meal.

We had tasty fixings here. I'm starting to think like the staff now. They say, "You in the South now!" Turkey, stuffing, my favorite sweet potatoes with marshmallows and brown sugar, green beans with crunchies on top, and some other yellow stuff. I ate three desserts and almost exploded after that.

Every day in chapel, we're supposed to sing with the music videos. Some of the songs are actually not bad, even though I miss my real music. The stuff that mom hated. I used to turn it up real loud whenever we got in the car so I didn't have to answer questions. Sometimes we'd have a battle over the radio knob. I always won, except when I let her win.

Wish I could talk to Ezra. I hope he won't forget the good times we had.

13

December 3

Mom and Dad are here, but I'm not allowed to see them yet. They have to meet with my teacher and Pastor Fred and take some kind of class.

Pastor Mitchell talked to me a lot this week. He reminds me of Dad. He's short and bald and has a pot belly and a foo man choo. Even his voice kind of sounds like Dad.

He helped me when I was feeling real sad one day. And on Friday, I was super mad because the millionaire kid is now tight with the kid who's always in my face daring me to do stuff. They're both out to get me.

I got so disgusted about everything. Pastor Mitchell was walking by and pulled me out of formation to go talk. I was glad because we were going to the weight room, and I was too tired to work out. Even a ten-minute break is better than nothing. Plus I like talking to him. I miss talking to Dad.

CADET,

It's "Fu Manchu."

- Pastor Fred

14

December 10

WHEW! Parent Visit was good! I miss everyone so much. But I'm still here. So that's pretty terrible. I hope they'll decide to bring me home for Christmas. I asked a whole lot, but didn't get anywhere with that.

I still can't put it in words about the visit. We played a lot of cards. I asked Dad to take a video of me talking, for Ezra. But it was hard to get through that. I hope he watches it anyway, because I know he is sad too.

We talked a whole lot — not much else to do if we have to stay on campus. We only had two arguments, and it was nothing like at home. It was weird that they have the power now and I can't really stick up for myself. They know they can say whatever they want and I have to just sit there and take it. All the counselors and Direct Care staff are on shift today because of Parent Visit, so watching eyeballs are everywhere.

Overall, it was a real good weekend. I didn't get the cheesesteak, but the subs they bought in town were good.

15

December 17

I've been here for over 100 days. When I was little in daycare, the 100 Days Party was a BIIGGG celebration.

Now I'm very, very sad. Christmas is almost here. I MISS EVERYONE. We get a seven-minute phone call home on December 25. That is all. NO presents.

School is strange. There's no real teacher here. This guy sits at a desk and we each have a little flag that we wave if we want to speak to him. He said he's a teacher, but I don't know any teacher like that!

Plus — no classes. Just workbooks. We sit for hours and my butt gets sore! The desks have a boring wall in front and boring walls on the sides, like a tiny jail cell. And how am I not supposed to look at anybody? I sit next to two kids: one is a weirdo and the other picks his nose.

The millionaire kid is three seats away — he can't reach me, but it's hard not to look at him when he's calling my name and making fun of my nose, my skin, my being short. I don't know why he has it in for me. He doesn't even know me.

I didn't like school at home, but at least I had some nice teachers and my friends around. Here is worse than being in jail. In jail, you get to sit around and do nothing if that is your desire.

CADET,

I understand where you're coming from. And this time of year can be quite sad for many people. I encourage you to come up with some positive things, no matter how small, to reflect upon this week.

- Pastor Fred

16

December 24

I wish Parent Visit was longer. Now it's like starting all over, and I won't see them for two more months. Mom keeps asking me if I made any friends. NO, MOM!

We go to chapel and have devotionals every day. Everyone's always telling us to keep our eyes and hearts on The Reason for The Season and all that. But it's CHRISTMAS EVE and I want to be home! I can't even talk to Ezra. Or Casey — she's on break from college.

I wonder if Mom put that funny Santa cup and cracked plate out. With milk and cookies. Overnight she pours the milk out so it looks like Santa drank it. And leaves a cookie with half a bite. I like that, like ol' Santa got too stuffed to take that one last nibble.

17

December 31

Christmas was very hard.

I wish I was home. And Ezra — we've had our fights over the years, but I miss him so much and can't wait to see him. I wonder if he's sad about me. If I could pick any brother in the world, I would pick him.

Everyone's talking about what happened Tuesday. Vasquez said a kid punched one of the Direct Cares in the head and attacked him, so the Direct Care ended up flipping the kid upside down and dropping him right on his head!

That is what they do here! I have never seen that personally, but that's what everyone says. Anyway, the Direct Care is HISTORY. So is the kid. My parents aren't going to like hearing this at all.

CADET,

The details of this are not accurate. Rise above, and do not be one who sows discord in others. Proverbs 6:19

– Pastor Fred

18

January 7

The holidays really shook a lot of us up. Some older guys were being really bad and aggressive, so the Direct Cares did Personal Restraint. It's kind of scary when you first see it. But not so much anymore.

The DCs are swole and they're always barking at us to stop messing around. Most of them have a bunch of tattoos and they wear black military pants and black boots and a black t-shirt.

When they do a Personal Restraint, they grab your arms behind you so you can't move too much.

If you try to head butt backwards you just end up with a sore neck. If you wrestle around it can hurt. That's what everyone says. I wouldn't know. I'm strong but not super big. Dad says because of my ethnicity I won't get very tall. Salvadorians are basically short. So I don't need to be getting into it with those dudes.

After that's all done, they might spend 5 or 10 minutes praying with the kid. Other boys come over and put their hands on the bad kids and pray too. Maybe like six people in all. I never saw THAT before, with a bunch of bullies, haha. But I'm getting used to that, too.

My birthday is coming up quickly. I asked Dad if I could get out by then, but he said no.

CADET,

The PR method is a state-approved technique used only when absolutely necessary. It's specifically designed for the effectiveness AND SAFETY of the assailant and those nearby. Parents of all incoming cadets have agreed to abide by this measure. It looks startling, but it's the best way to defuse these types of situations.

– Pastor Fred

19

January 14

I don't know what to say today. It's been quiet this week. Pastor Fred left and everyone is feeling sad.

He got a job in North Santi. The staff is saying when you have five kids, you have to make enough money to put food on the table. He was my counselor, so I am especially sad.

Things I need for second Parent Visit:

6 bottles of shampoo

4 pairs of socks

My Stormtrooper slippers

My cell phone!

I gave three shampoo bottles to this kid who said he didn't have any more. And then I lost some. So I only have one. Mom was suspicious, I think. She asked why I needed more because the nine bottles she gave me were supposed to last 18 months.

What's wrong with helping a person out? I get shot down whenever I try to do something nice. She was always getting on me at home because she thinks I try to buy friendships by giving people stuff. Wrong, Mom!

Schrodinger, that kid, has been bugging me again. Now he's calling me "taco bender" and "dumb wet." But he always does it when the Direct Cares aren't watching. I got written up for tripping him at lunch.

20

January 21

It's my birthday next week.

Dinner was excellent. Mrs. T-Bone makes a really good hamburger. She puts secret ingredients in it. No offense to Mom, but Mrs. T's burgers are way better than hers.

The chow hall ladies are nice. If you really like a certain food, they might give you extra. On Sundays we're allowed to get seconds if we want to. I always get seconds of everything, even if I don't eat it.

There was another fight in barracks last night. I am glad I have the end bunk. Some of these boys are in twelfth grade. When they fight it's like those MMA guys on TV, only it's three feet away.

My teacher told me I mess around too much. What does that mean?! I see all these really bad kids here. A lot worse than me.

Mr. Todd (a Direct Care) is cool. He lived in New York and he knows Big Bubba's Steak Shop!! I could go for a Spiedie sandwich right this second.

Two more weeks until Parent Weekend. Maybe Mom and Dad can get me a meat lover's pizza when they come.

CADET,

I won't be here on Thursday. Happy Birthday to you.

– Pastor Gabe

21

January 28

Today is MY BIRTHDAY!!! So bummed I have to spend it here.

I should be home so I could get presents and Dad could take me and my friends to race mini-cars and go to Rio 8 for sno-cones and subs. It's different here.

Mrs. T-Bone made me a big cake with my name on it. It was pretty tasty. They made me give a speech to thank people in my life. I was so nervous I don't even remember what I said.

HAPPY BIRTHDAYYYY TOOOOO MEEEEEEE (15). Worst birthday ever. No — I take that back. The worst was my thirteenth, when I only had three kids to invite and none of them showed.

Vasquez is gone. I don't know why he left. A few weeks ago, he told me that this place is super expensive and his parents were running out of money. So maybe that is why. I kind of miss him. I didn't even get to say goodbye.

Three guys got in trouble this week. They were in the bathroom making homemade tattoos with a paper clip. I'm not sure where they got ink. They had to call their parents and confess. Sanders said his mom was super trippin'. His tattoo looked so bad. Yep, it looked like a paper clip did it!

I'm about to explode. The millionaire kid called me Juan Valdez and said, "Why don't you go pick some coffee beans?" ONE OF THESE DAYS.

CADET,

Threats are forbidden. We will talk to the other cadet about the name-calling.

– Pastor Gabe

P.S.

I got called names too. You know my last name is Hernandez, right? We'll discuss at session.

22

February 4

GOOD VISIT with MA and PA! We played basketball a lot. And Monopoly all three days. Dad and I like to wheel and deal a lot, but Mom only wants to play by the exact rules so she's usually out first.

Parents go to chapel with us on Sunday. It's packed, like 300 people. Everyone is singing and it is so loud that it almost lifts you up off your feet. That, and the speakers are really loud so the bass is thumping in your chest.

Mom looks like she needs to work out. Her muffin top is getting bigger! Dad looks very tired. I am sad 'cause he has some medical problems. I get afraid that he will die before I come home. I love my Dad. He is my best friend.

23

February 11

Dad said I should think about my goals in life. So here they are:

1.   I want baller shoes — Nike LeBron 15 — to add to my collection! They are like $185. Mom

will say they're too expensive. She should mind her own biz and not butt in mine

1. $100 gift card to Circle K so I can get food whenever I want and not have to rely on anyone else to pay

1.   Be a pro baseball player and make $1,000,000,000,000

1.   Go HOME

There's a bunch more but I am tired of writing it all.

I asked Mom and Dad if I could come home. It's like the twentieth time I asked. Because we had 20 phone calls. I think when they come here it will be easier to show them that I'm good now and that I can come home and be better.

24

February 18

    I got written up for giving away some socks. Sucks! PUNISHED for nothing. Mom's always yapping that I don't need friends who want me for my stuff. What does she know? I have my friends at home and I don't need any here.

More new kids. I must be getting used to this place because the orientation doesn't shock me anymore. They make you wear an ugly old jumpsuit with ORIENTATION written in big letters on the back. For two weeks! And you have to wear socks and slaps, so it's hard to run away.

When you first arrive, the Direct Cares make you sleep on a mat for two weeks in the middle of the room. I didn't get much sleep. They try to wear you out by making you do all these exercises and running and marching in the hot sun but my mind still raced at night.

P.S. I almost got heat stroke

CADET,

You and your parents have been advised that if the weather is extreme, precautions are taken so no one gets overheated.

– Pastor Gabe

25

February 25

I couldn't sleep last night, thinking about all the times I pushed Mom around. I am basically a happy person but she was always doing things that made me so angry — getting in my stuff and messing it up, like my backpack and in my closet. I don't know how she always seemed to know when I was hiding things or stole something. Dad was usually clueless. And she would always call me out on it, which really ticked me off.

But when I think about the times I shoved her around and maybe punched her, it kind of makes me sick. Once I hit her with the wiffle ball bat. It was hard plastic and I thought she'd move out of the way when I swung it.

I hope she can forgive me. When I get back, I hope they can try hard to judge when I'm about to lose it, and everyone can back off and calm down.

Another boy left on Sunday. He wore the graduation robe and after chapel he got his high school certificate and made a speech about how this place changed his life. I couldn't believe it — he turned 18 in January but he stuck around to finish school. He coulda signed himself out two months ago!

Pastor Mitchell looked like he was crying a little. Maybe Mr. Todd, too. The kid's family was there and after everyone prayed over him they whisked him away. I wanted to be him! Then I would be OUT!!

26

March 4

A kid in Daniel platoon snuck on a computer in the main office, but they caught him and now he has bathroom cleaning detail. Plus he got kicked back to Jacob platoon. They call it that because the name means Deceiver. That is where I am.

When I get four good evaluations in a row I'm gonna ask to get on kitchen detail. I took Food Science in eighth grade so I already know how to make burritos and homemade mac n' cheese.

I DON'T want laundry detail. All that stinko underwear. No thanks, bro.

It's weird. I feel like I know this place really well now. A little guy who arrived today was shaking like a leaf. I remember that. You come in all scared, you don't know what's happening. They take you to this room and pat you down and make you take your clothes off and put on the jumpsuit, and then they take you to the barber shop room to shave your head with #1 clippers.

One kid's been here over two years. That's like half his life! I can't say too much because my counselor said all these rules for what you're allowed to write. But I know what I am thinking!! He said his dad was a drunk and beat him up a lot. And then the dad got sick and died. I feel kind of sorry for the kid. But not too much. I don't want to be making any friends here.

27

March 11

Pastor Fred used to say that all people are valuable and worthy in the EYES of GOD. And that it is PEOPLE who make the bad choice and say some are less worthy.

Mom keeps saying I'm Latino. But I feel more like Black. I never really knew any Latinos before I got here.

There were about 20 Black kids in my classes back home, and I knew them all.

Everybody [Mom and Dad, counselors, teachers here and at home] wants me to EXPLORE my birth and stuff. I've been hearing that for years. Why would I want to do that? I don't even remember it.

28

March 18

Here's all I know:

- My real mom is Josefina Juana Flores and she gave birth to me but was really poor and worked in a factory that made fertilizer for growing stuff, and she didn't have a phone or address —

just a dirt road in a rural village.

- My real dad is Izan Santiago and he's a lot older than my mom, and he left right away and never saw me.

- His whereabouts are unknown. That's what it said on the paperwork.

- I ended up in an orphanage until I was four, even though I'm not an orphan.

Then Mom and Dad flew over there and got me. Dad always tells people I cried every night for a long time after that.

And that's all, folks!

29

March 25

Yay for me! Four good evaluations in a row — so tomorrow I start kitchen detail. I hope I get to cook some burritos.

Been thinking about my El Salvador mom. I tried really hard, but I don't remember her. Someday I'm gonna go back and find her. I never met my dad, but I miss having a real dad... like, who is he? Do I look like him? How am I ever gonna find him? Maybe my mom will know how.

Two older guys got caught drinking the blue water that has the combs in it, in the barbershop. My counselor said it has alcohol in it. And those guys were desperate. I can't even imagine putting that in my mouth. Probably tasted horrible and had a bunch of hairs in it. I would spit it out on the floor. Dumb guys.

P.S. I have a friend. He reminds me so much of Ezra. He's two years older than me. I can talk to him whenever I feel bad and he really helps me a lot. He's also funny like Ezra.

30

April 1

It was really good to see Dad and Mom (this was the third time). Mrs. T-Bone let us use utensils and stuff to have a cookout on the grill. Mom had to be with me when we got it and returned it. Plus I wasn't allowed to touch the knife the whole time. It's real strict here.

I also can't hold Mom's or Dad's cell phones, and they can't buy me any energy drinks. And I can't go near their rental car. What am I gonna do, jump in and race away? I haven't even taken Driver's Ed!

Mom did that April Fool trick where you attach a string to a dollar bill and then lay the dollar on the floor and when someone tries to grab it, you jerk the string. She put it on the basketball court and I completely fell for it. Oh well, what would I do with money here?

On Saturday I told them I was afraid that when I got back home, things would go back to the way they were. So I asked if they could watch for signs that I was getting real mad, and then back off.

Mom did that unblinking stare. Finally, she said it wasn't their job to do that. I couldn't believe it! How are things gonna get better if they won't help me?

She said it was up to me to learn to handle my emotions, and not lose control. If I could do that, I would have done it ALL ALONG! I was so upset, I asked them to take me back to the barracks. I was still mad the next day so Dad called Pastor Gabe over and he agreed with Mom and Dad. But they're wrong!

CADET,

Temper is an extremely hard emotion to control. Trust me, I've been there. Proverbs 25:28 says "A man without self-control is like a city broken into and left without walls." When you let your anger get the best of you, it's likely YOU who receives most of the fallout. I mean, look where you are. We'll keep working on it during sessions.

– Pastor Gabe

31

April 8

Yesterday was SUPER DOPE!!! Some of us who are doing really well got to go to the beach. The water was amazing! Warm and blue/green. You could even see little fish swimming around your legs. The sand was white like sugar.

We threw a tennis ball around in the water. Guess who tried to bean me with the ball? I tried to bean him back but Pastor Mitchell broke it up. He made us sit on the concrete ledge for 20 minutes. I am starting to realize that nothing I say or do to the jerk ever does me any good. My good friend told me to chill and pretend the guy doesn't exist. But I sure don't like him just getting away with crap.

There were tons of tiny creatures called sand fleas that crawled around our feet at the water. Pastor Mitchell said we should fry them up and have a flea tasting. I just might have eaten them. I really miss all that Greasy Fried Goodness. But we ended up getting pizza and a big tub of GREASY FRENCH FRIES! So good.

When I went to bed I could still feel the waves on my body.

32

April 15

We have a new counselor. He's kind of strange. And funny! He said he is a Rabbi which is like a Pastor, only Jewish. And we can call him Reb Avi. He told us about who he is and why he's here, but I was so tired that I didn't catch a lot of it. He said he is on loan from God for a few months, haha.

I was tired because three kids ran away Tuesday overnight. There was a mad rush at 4 a.m. when someone noticed. It was cool — all these cops raced up in their cars and so we didn't have to do morning devotionals.

It took 36 hours to find them. They were in the swamps two miles away. They were really hot and just sitting in the shade. Good thing no alligators came by!

The Direct Cares told us that there is no place to run. And that people who live around here can tell by our clothes who we are and call the police. Then you're back in a jumpsuit doing bathroom cleaning detail until you're 80 years old.

Plus you have to stay a month longer in the program.

33

April 22

A kid hurled all over the floor by his bunk today. The whole place reeks. Glad I didn't have to clean it up.

I feel bad for some stuff I did to Mom and Dad. I took a ton of money. I gave a lot of it away. And I bought all kinds of stuff: cell phone, Xbox games, food, another skateboard. Plus I gave a bunch of Mom's jewelry to my friends. But she hardly ever wore it anyway.

Pastor Gabe said we need to keep talking about it. So I guess that will happen. He's an okay guy. I know you are reading this, PASTOR GABRIEL!!!

He is from Porto Rico so he knows what I am dealing with in this place. He says when someone says my skin looks like sh-- or things like that, I should let it roll off my back and also ask God to help me not get so angry.

CADET,

I'm actually from Dallas. My parents are from Puerto Rico. And yes, we will talk in session.

– Pastor Gabe

34

April 29

This is like the 1,000th time that kid was abusing me. I am ON THE EDGE!! He is back in a jumpsuit but still!!!

They try to keep us apart, but we're in the same platoon so it's nearly impossible. I still have my end bunk, and they moved him to the opposite end. I'm glad they didn't move me. The big snorers are on the other side.

My friend says there will always be people in this world who don't like you. And that even Mother Teresa, who's like a saint, probably had a few enemies.

He told me that some older boys bullied him when he first got here. But after his second time being put back in a jumpsuit after some fights, he remembered that when he was at home, HE had picked on other kids in his school. So he figured this was his payback in life.

He said he's tired of the bully life. He said in elementary school they taught prevention techniques that he thought were dumb, but now he's trying one. If someone is saying nasty stuff to you, grab those words flying through the air before they reach you, and stuff them into a mental garbage can. I don't think that's going to work for me but because my friend said it, I'll try.

35

May 6

A kid two bunks down from me said Mr. Todd stomped on his foot with his boot and broke his toe. No one saw him do that, so it's the kid's word against his. Mr. Todd does not seem like a person who would do that.

But it's a classic way to get your parents to feel bad and yank you out of here. I know at least two dozen ways to accomplish that. I've already tried a bunch but Mom & Dad are not budging, which is surprising to me. At home I could make them do almost anything.

Reb Avi started Anger Class on Thursdays. We don't have to go but we get bonus points on our weekly evaluations if we do. Last night this kid cried when he talked about his best friend who killed himself. He said it was last year and he tries not to think about it, but he ends up thinking about it all the time.

I just listen... even when they try to get me to talk. I'm not spilling my guts in front of that crowd!

36

May 13

In our phone call this week, Mom brought up all this stuff I did. She just can't leave the past alone. All that is ancient history. She said this program says to have the "Hard Conversations." I don't know why, though.

She asked if I ever did drugs, because I always said I'd never do that. She tricked me! She didn't say she had already looked through my cell phone and found that old video of me smoking weed in the car with Dominic and his squad. I only did it like three times. Dominic did it twice a day!

Plus she asked if I smashed her old cell phone and tossed it in the garbage can. Sheesh, Mom! Whaddya digging around in the trash for?!

CADET,

Parents are encouraged to have these hard conversations with their sons. It's a vital part of your growth as a young man entering adulthood. I do see your point of view in that it's not always productive to dwell on yesterday's hurts and challenges. We can discuss in session and also when your parents come.

– Pastor Gabe

37

May 20

I could barely stay awake in devotionals this morning. I kept zoning out and plus it was kinda boring. I like it when Pastor Gabe leads devotionals 'cause he keeps it real. He is out today because his wife is having a baby.

Yesterday it was about Daniel in the lion's den. Pastor Gabe said God will protect his worshipers even when they're facing possible death. Like he made the lions keep their jaws shut. We saw a video about it. It was wild. I like a lot of the videos, especially the ones where they have epic battles.

Pastor Gabe said his parents smoked weed all the time when he was growing up. He said he wasted a lot of years and got in a lot of trouble before he got straightened out. He was in a program like this one only for grownups, in Florida.

I finished 15 workbooks and memorized the codes of honor and some Psalms. I'm up for a big promotion. When I get it, I can move to Daniel platoon. It's cool because it's mostly older boys and not as rowdy. AND I get to ditch the school workbooks and go on the computer. I'll get extra privileges — don't know what they are, but they must be pretty special.

The hard part is that you have to stand before the boards — some are staff and the rest are boys — and they vote on you. It's nerve-wracking.

38

May 27

CRAP. I got turned down by boards yesterday. I was so nervous. I passed all my written and oral stuff. But I got voted down. They said I was too much in everybody's faces. And not showing consistency in behavior. Sucks.

Last night I was thinking about Charlie, my best friend for three years. I practically lived at his house, which made Mom annoyed. And sad. His family was awesome and their food was so much better, like sausage sticks and potato chips. Plus a fridge in the basement packed with sodas that you could take whenever.

I wanted to be in their family in the worst way. I did some bad stuff at their house but always got away with it. But right after fifth grade I said something bad (it was a lie anyway!) to Charlie and his sister, so his Mom called my Mom and I never went over there anymore. Then they moved. I hardly ever thought about him after that so I'm wondering, why am I thinking about him now?

CADET,

There's a saying I've learned the hard way: Never give the devil a ride 'cause he'll want to take over the driving. If you want to talk more about this, my ears are waiting for you.

– Pastor Gabe

39

June 3

Dad and Mom are coming tomorrow. I'm going to ask them if I can grow my hair out on top when I get home. I'm tired of getting shaved every week! Yesterday the #2 clippers broke so I had to get the #1 — you can really see my scar from when I was fighting that neighbor kid and his teeth hit my head. Mom stayed with me for six hours in the ER that night and I got five stitches but no rabies, haha.

I have to remember to show Mom what I'm reading. It's a series and it's really good. Mom tries to get whatever I read out of the library at home so she can talk about it with me.

Dad's gonna bring some pictures of the new development he's working on. I know he'd like me to go into the business someday. I don't know if I'm a college kind of guy, but I don't know if I want to build houses either. I just don't know yet!

40

June 10

I went before boards and got turned down AGAIN. Same old reasons, plus more. Bennigan has it in for me. He said I was sneaky. He should talk! He's always bragging about how he's gonna get drunk and party when he gets out of here.

Last weekend was cool, though. Dad's photos were impressive. He's really a good designer and builder. Sometimes I wish I could work with him, but first we'd have to figure out a way to be together without all the yelling and stuff.

Most of the boys that came in when I did have overnight off-campus privileges now. We were all bad, but I guess I messed up too much all along. But... some of those guys are sneaky and they just don't get caught.

CADET,

If you work hard and make it to Daniel Platoon, you may earn an off-campus pass by August. You need to stop messing around, though. We're looking for consistency and integrity. Those are the things that keep holding you back. And don't concern yourself with anyone else. You take charge of you.

– Pastor Gabe

41

June 17

More new kids. One has been a handful. He's been here two weeks and already he's been in like 10 fights. The first night he cut some holes in his mattress. I saw the knife when Pastor Mitchell took it away from him. It was cool — tiny with swirly colors on it. I can't figure out how he got it in here. I guess they don't strip-search the newbs anymore.

I really like working in the kitchen. The cook ladies are so nice. I found out that Mrs. T-Bone's real name is Mrs. León! In a weird way, it's almost like a family here. A family of chefs, haha.

I didn't like cooking at home. Mom would look over my shoulder saying I needed more of this or that, like a spice. She said she was just trying to give me tips. But I already knew how to cook. I am FAMOUS for my scrambled eggs here.

I have a nickname now. Most of the guys do. When they found out my first name they started calling me Maxwell House. Then Cuppa Joe. Then Decaf. They wrote D. Caff on tape and stuck it to my locker. So any of those.

42

June 24

Super mad today.

I don't feel like writing.

You-know-who called me names so I socked him in the gut. I couldn't help it. Plus I got "Having No Integrity" and "Failure to Follow" deductions on my weekly evaluation because I talked back to Mr. Janson when he broke us up. I was mad all week and didn't do so good in school and ended up with a FAIL for the week.

All because of ONE JERK. I think this whole place is just out to get me. Mom and Dad had better take me home on next visit. Mr. Todd gave me seven points off because he said I disrespected him in a threatening way. Nah bro. He gave ME the stink eye first. I guess they expect you to be perfect, like a robot who does whatever it's told even if it's unfair or dumb.

This means I won't get to go before boards this week. So I'm done. THAT IS ALL.

CADET,

You've been told many times, it's up to you how you want your life to play out. We (and your parents and teachers) are here to guide you, help you, encourage you, comfort you... but YOU are the one who must make the decisions and do the hard work. Life isn't always easy or fair. But you are not being singled out. We all deal with that. Rise above, son. Make a conscious effort to act honorably, and you'll find that things will fall into place much more easily.

– Pastor Gabe

43

July 1

Starting to feel really bad about all the $$ I stole. Mom knew it way back, and it used to make me so mad that she knew. I had to lie to cover my tracks. She kept pressing me all the time and would make a big deal out of counting money in wallets.

I lied so much that it was almost like it became the truth. I don't know if I realized it until lately — that I lied about almost everything. Even stupid stuff like, "Where's that green jacket?" I would say anything just to end a conversation.

I told Pastor Mitchell about all this yesterday and was so relieved to finally get it off my chest. I hope everyone forgives me. When I think about how much I stole, WOW, I could have bought a car with all that money.

44

July 8

It was the best of times, it was the worst of times. That's what Dad says sometimes. It's from a book. He said that in high school I'll probably have to read it.

That saying came into my mind because:

GOOD: It's PARENT WEEKEND

BAD: I was turned down AGAIN at boards

It's been real good to have Dad and Mom here, and it mostly keeps my mind off things. On the phone they sometimes sound frustrated with me, but in person they have been nice and supportive. Especially Dad.

We had lots of good food this weekend. The soft ice cream machine in the chow hall is finally working so we all had chocolate and vanilla striped cones. TWICE.

I still am not allowed to see Ezra or Casey. I have to get two promotions for that.

I got turned down by boards and this time everyone voted against me. As much I tried not to, I cried. One kid said I was two-faced, like I act one way around the staff and another way behind their backs. Another kid said I still lie. Who doesn't! And most all of them said I didn't show consistency in behavior. I'm so sick of hearing that.

45

July 15

Reb Avi is a trip. He says funny things and kind of raps it: "We are not here to SCARE you. We are here to PRE-PARE you. Can I get an Amen on that?" And "Being a man ain't got nothing to do with age. You can be a boy until you go to your grave, depraved."

Last week he showed clips of two movies. The first was *The Sound of Music* where the nanny lady runs around all happy and dancing and singing. The second one was *Saving Private Ryan*, when they're in a battle and there are soldiers on fire who have been shot and there's bloody gore and throwing up and guys shaking and crying.

Then he said, "This is what we grow up thinking life is supposed to be" (the nanny singing). "But this," (the second movie) "is what life is like. Gentlemen, YOU are in a BATTLE. And you BETTER SUIT UP."

CADET,

:-)

- Pastor Gabe

46

July 22

YES!!! I got promoted!!! It's ONLY been over two months since I've been trying, haha.

So COOL. I get to go to Daniel platoon. It's a lot roomier, and the Direct Cares aren't in there 24/7 so it's more relaxed. And my good friend (who reminds me of

Ezra) is there. I can't wait to move my stuff over. PLUS it's away from the jerk!

I'm still behind in school. But it doesn't really matter because we have school all year. I'm working on Science and English, but they're really hard. Workbook 6 is all about sentences and diagrams. Who needs that in real life?! I am going to be a baseball player. And after that, maybe a video game designer. And make a ton of $$$. I'll just need to know Math so I can calculate how many millions I'll have.

47

July 29

In Anger Class, Reb Avi talked about all different kinds of anger. He said there were Exploding Time Bombs (out of control) and Calculated Time Bombs (in control). I never thought about it before. Mom used to say I was out of control a lot. But after hearing this, I think I was trying to BE in control a lot. So who knows. It makes me confused to think about it too much.

My good friend is going to do the water baptism at next Parent Visit. Crazy! We've been having some long talks. He told me the way to deal with guys like Schrodinger is to act like they don't exist. Don't answer back, don't look at him, don't allow him to take up your air. Just... play a song in your head that you like. I'm trying, even though I just want to flatten him.

48

August 5

Mom and Dad are here — it's their fifth Parent Visit, not counting when they brought me here. I guess it's pretty expensive for them to come. The plane ride, the rental car, the hotel, the food. Plus Dad has to take off work and sometimes his boss doesn't want him to.

TOP 10 THINGS WE DID THIS WEEKEND:

1.   Ate

1.   Played basketball

1.   Showed Mom and Dad what we do in the weight room

1.   Had a baseball catch

1.   Played pool

1.   Looked at the new vocational building

1.   Watched my friend get baptized in a big tub of water

1.   Skipped rocks on the pond

1.   Ate

1.   Taught Mom and Dad Hebrew: *toda raba* means "thank you very much"

We talked about when I go home. Mom said I will have to earn the right to have a flip phone. Come on!

That's for old people! There's not even internet on it. Or texting. I'm gonna have to do something about that.

Wild Boys

49

August 12

LOTS OF ACTION TODAY! We played kickball, only the bases were blow-up kiddie pools and the base paths were slip-n-slides. It was awesome. You couldn't run without slipping around. We were all laughing so hard. Then we had a cookout and cupcakes.

The only bad thing was You-Know-Who. We were beating his team. So he squirted me with the hose. On purpose. Right in my eyes! I think my eyes were open. It hurt so bad.

But it makes no sense what he did next. I don't even like to recall it but he said some terrible stuff about how Mom and Dad are white and I'm not. He kept dropping the f-bomb and the other kids kind of froze because they knew we were being supervised.

I couldn't help it — I charged him. But at the last second something stopped me. My fist was in the air and I was shaking it in his face. He shoved me down and that hurt a little. But the sting was really in his words.

Mr. Todd and Reb Avi both saw it and broke us up. Mr. Todd made us go into the chow hall and tell our sides of the story. Then he sent me back outside, but I haven't seen the kid since.

50

August 19

I've been thinking about that incident a whole lot. Trying to figure out why I didn't lay that guy out. I could have. I would have, last year. Maybe it was the technique my best friend told me about. Plus — I really want to see my bro! It's been almost a year since I talked to him. I knew if I lost it on the guy, I'd FAIL my evaluation for sure.

AND it's always me who gets in trouble. I just didn't want to deal with all that this time around.

Some of us from Daniel platoon went off campus to this old folks' home. I'm not sure how two hours will change their life, but some of them seemed glad to see us. We sang some of our chapel songs and Reb Avi played piano.

Then we had to talk to the people and pray with them. It was a little weird, but I picked out a guy who looked like a nice grandpa and we got along okay. He thought he knew me but I never met him before. Reb Avi says it's never too late — even at 80! — to have a transformation, same as what they want for us.

The best part is we went out to a restaurant after that. We could get whatever we wanted. At home I would always order two meals and a giant soda, and Dad would be totally cool but Mom would go into a fit. But I'm trying to work on my six-pack abs now so I can't be ordering all that.

It was a good day. Pastor Gabe said he's seeing good changes in me.

51

August 26

    It's my Grandma's birthday today. She would be... I forget. Like 90 or something! She was the best. She would look all over New York to find me the exact presents I asked for. And she always had our favorite cereal when we stayed at her house. Mom didn't like that because the cereal had marshmallows in it and Ezra and I would eat three bowls at a time. I guess I did get pretty revved up.

When Grandma got cancer she changed, and it was really sad. I wanted her to live so badly that I prayed and said if God made her better, I would be a good boy. I was little then.

I miss her a lot. Mom always lights a candle on her birthday even though she liked her own mom best. Grandma was really religious and would always say, "Praise the Lord," and wave her hand in the air. Like, maybe a little too much. I guess she made it to the streets of gold — that's what she always called heaven.

I just realized yesterday that my friend here who reminds me of Ezra is my best friend now. I never really had a best friend. I mean one who liked me for me. I bought kids a lot of stuff. I did CRAZY things I never should have done. It makes me burn (embarrassment and anger) to think about that. Sometimes my buds put me down when they were asking me to do stuff for them.

I guess Charlie from my kid years was my best friend. But I wasn't his. It used to make me so mad. I remember trying to get back at some of those kids he hung around with.

CADET,

We think of that kind of prayer as divine blackmail. Don't bargain with God or give Him an ultimatum. He always hears and answers, even if it's not the answer we wanted to hear. We'll never (on this earth) know why things happen as they do. Just trust that God's love is everlasting.

- Pastor Gabe

Wild Boys

52

September 2

I counted all the Latino guys who are in the program right now. Here's what I found:

14 – Hispanic (that I know of)

8 – Black

2 – Asian

1 – Indian

6 – Mixed or I can't exactly tell

' There are about 75 boys here so I probably missed a few.

But almost 20% are Latino. Pastor Gabe is, too. So is Mrs. T-Bone's husband. And her four kids. And the new Direct Care guy. So I'm in good company here. If those two jerks are going to keep at it, they should know they're also disrespecting the people who feed them and counsel them and keep their smelly underwear clean.

Plus if you count the other boys (8, 2, 1, 6 — above) I know for a fact that some of them are picked on, especially the newer and younger ones.

CADET,

You're starting to recognize how it is in the world. Hatred and racism will always exist in some form. The key is to keep focusing on the light. "The light shines in the darkness, and the darkness comprehends it not." (John

1:5) If you're not sure what that means, we can discuss in session.

– Pastor Gabe

53

September 9

I've been here a year! Can't believe I only have six months to go. I'll be back home by spring. Hopefully I can take Driver's Ed then. Awesome.

Best of all — I get to see Ezra and Casey in three weeks!! I have an off-campus pass for five whole days! I can't wait.

My friend who reminds me so much of Ezra left yesterday. He's real smart, so he graduated from the program AND from high school. His family invited me to eat with them in the chow hall on Friday night. They are really nice, but I probably won't ever see them again because they're from Utah and I'm from New York.

On Sunday when they had his graduation ceremony in chapel, everyone surrounded him and his family and prayed over them. I couldn't help it — I was crying during that, and then in my bunk that afternoon. And last night.

He told me right before he left that he was passing the baton on to me. That it was my journey now, to carry on in a good way and to help other kids, too.

I don't know if I'm ready for that. But what have I got to lose?

About The Author

Kat Jeanette resides outside of Philadelphia, PA. Though new to fiction writing, she has written in other formats, including nonfiction essay and advertising copywriting.

About The Publisher

Story Shares is a nonprofit focused on supporting the millions of teens and adults who struggle with reading by creating a new shelf in the library specifically for them. The ever-growing collection features content that is compelling and culturally relevant for teens and adults, yet still readable at a range of lower reading levels.

Story Shares generates content by engaging deeply with writers, bringing together a community to create this new kind of book. With more intriguing and approachable stories to choose from, the teens and adults who have fallen behind are improving their skills and beginning to discover the joy of reading. For more information, visit storyshares.org.

Easy to Read. Hard to Put Down.

www.ingramcontent.com/pod-product-compliance
Lightning Source LLC
Chambersburg PA
CBHW051254170626
46809CB00004B/1643